Bertie
and the Big
Balloon

First published in 2007 by
Franklin Watts
338 Euston Road
London
NW1 3BH

Franklin Watts Australia
Level 17/207 Kent Street
Sydney
NSW 2000

A CIP catalogue record for this book is available
from the British Library.

ISBN 978 0 7496 7161 7 (hbk)
ISBN 978 0 7496 7305 5 (pbk)

Series Editor: Jackie Hamley
Editor: Melanie Palmer
Series Advisor: Dr Hilary Minns
Series Designer: Peter Scoulding

Printed in China

Franklin Watts is a division of
Hachette Children's Books.

Bertie
and the Big
Balloon

by Sue Graves

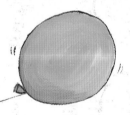

Illustrated by Helen Jackson

W
FRANKLIN WATTS
LONDON•SYDNEY

Sue Graves

"I'd love to fly up in the air on a big balloon. But I wouldn't like getting stuck in a tree like poor Bertie!".

Helen Jackson

"I love this book because the idea of flying with a HUGE balloon is BRILLIANT! I wish it would happen to me!"

Mum got Bertie
a big balloon.

It went up and up.

Bertie went up and up.

"Come down!"
said Mum.

"I can't," said Bertie.
"I'm flying!"

The balloon went over Gran's house.

"Come down!"
said Gran.

"I can't," said Bertie.
"I'm flying!"

The balloon hit a tree.

"Come down!"
said everyone.

"I can't," said Bertie.
"I'm stuck!"

Dad got Bertie down.

"Can I have a new balloon?" Bertie asked.

"No!" said everyone.

Notes for adults

TADPOLES are structured to provide support for newly independent readers. The stories may also be used by adults for sharing with young children.

Starting to read alone can be daunting. **TADPOLES** help by providing visual support and repeating words and phrases. These books will both develop confidence and encourage reading and rereading for pleasure.

If you are reading this book with a child, here are a few suggestions:

1. Make reading fun! Choose a time to read when you and the child are relaxed and have time to share the story.
2. Talk about the story before you start reading. Look at the cover and the blurb. What might the story be about? Why might the child like it?
3. Encourage the child to reread the story, and to retell the story in their own words, using the illustrations to remind them what has happened.
4. Discuss the story and see if the child can relate it to their own experience, or perhaps compare it to another story they know.
5. Give praise! Remember that small mistakes need not always be corrected.

If you enjoyed this book, why not try another TADPOLES story?